THE GREAT HOLIDAY COOKIE SWAP

MELANIE M. KYER   ILLUSTRATED BY JOE KULKA

PELICAN PUBLISHING
NEW ORLEANS 2020

The word "Pelican" and the depiction of a pelican are trademarks of Arcadia Publishing Company Inc. and are registered in the U.S. Patent and Trademark Office.

Library of Congress Cataloging-in-Publication Data

Names: Kyer, Melanie M., author. | Kulka, Joe, illustrator.
Title: The great holiday cookie swap/ Melanie M. Kyer ; illustrated by Joe Kulka.
Description: New Orleans : Pelican Publishing, 2020. | Summary: Told in rhyming text, eight different cookies from different cultures get together at the December Swap party, and argue over who is the best, tastiest cookie. Includes recipes and facts about traditional cookies from different countries.
Identifiers: LCCN 2019042450 | ISBN 9781455625239 (hardback) | ISBN 9781455625246 (ebook)
Subjects: LCSH: Cookies—Juvenile fiction. | Ethnic food—Juvenile fiction. | Stories in rhyme. | CYAC: Stories in rhyme. | Cookies—Fiction. | Ethnic food—Fiction. | LCGFT: Stories in rhyme. | Humorous fiction.
Classification: LCC PZ8.3.K982 Gr 2020 | DDC [E]—dc23
LC record available at https://lccn.loc.gov/2019042450

Printed in Malaysia

Published by Pelican Publishing
New Orleans, LA
www.pelicanpub.com

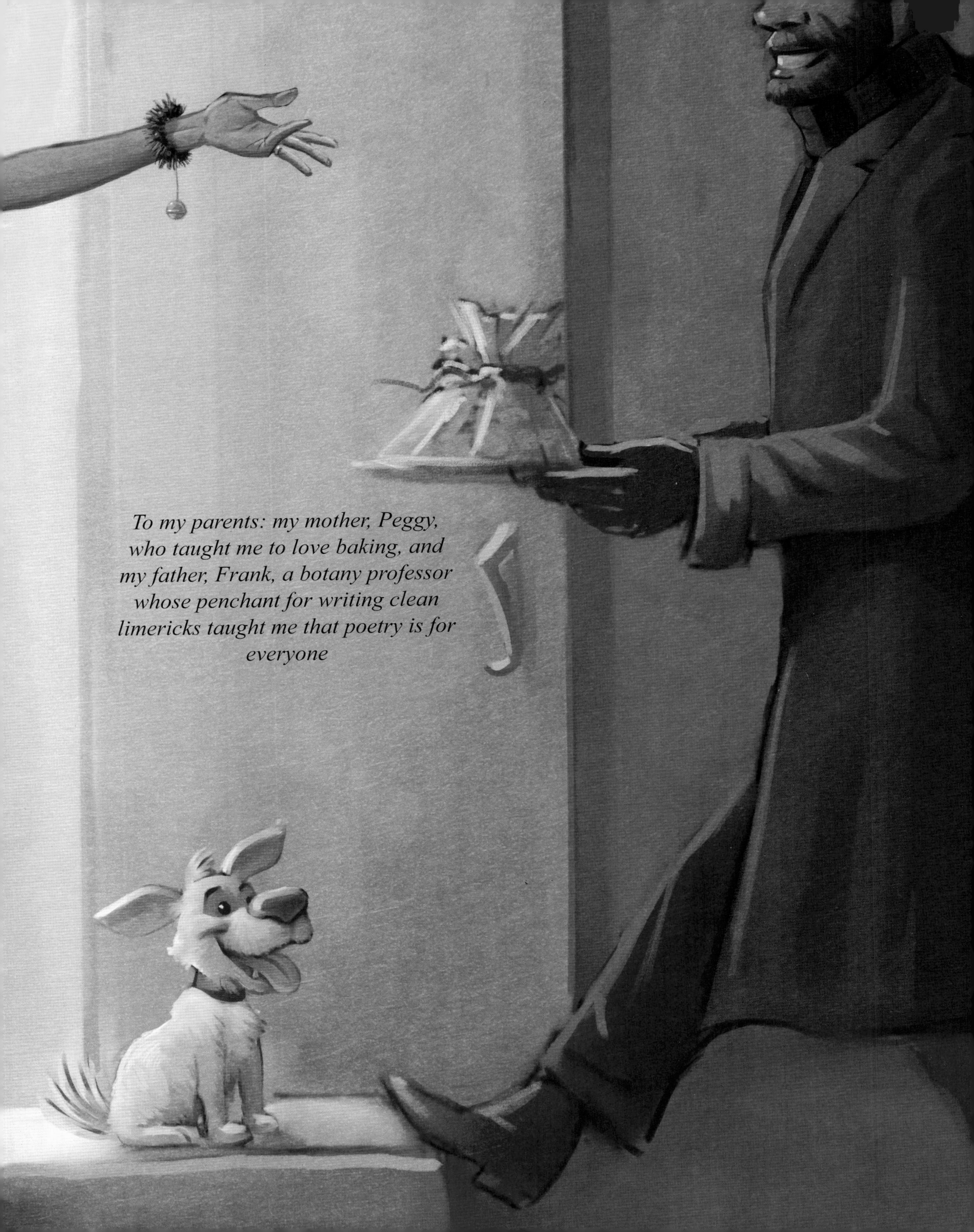

To my parents: my mother, Peggy, who taught me to love baking, and my father, Frank, a botany professor whose penchant for writing clean limericks taught me that poetry is for everyone

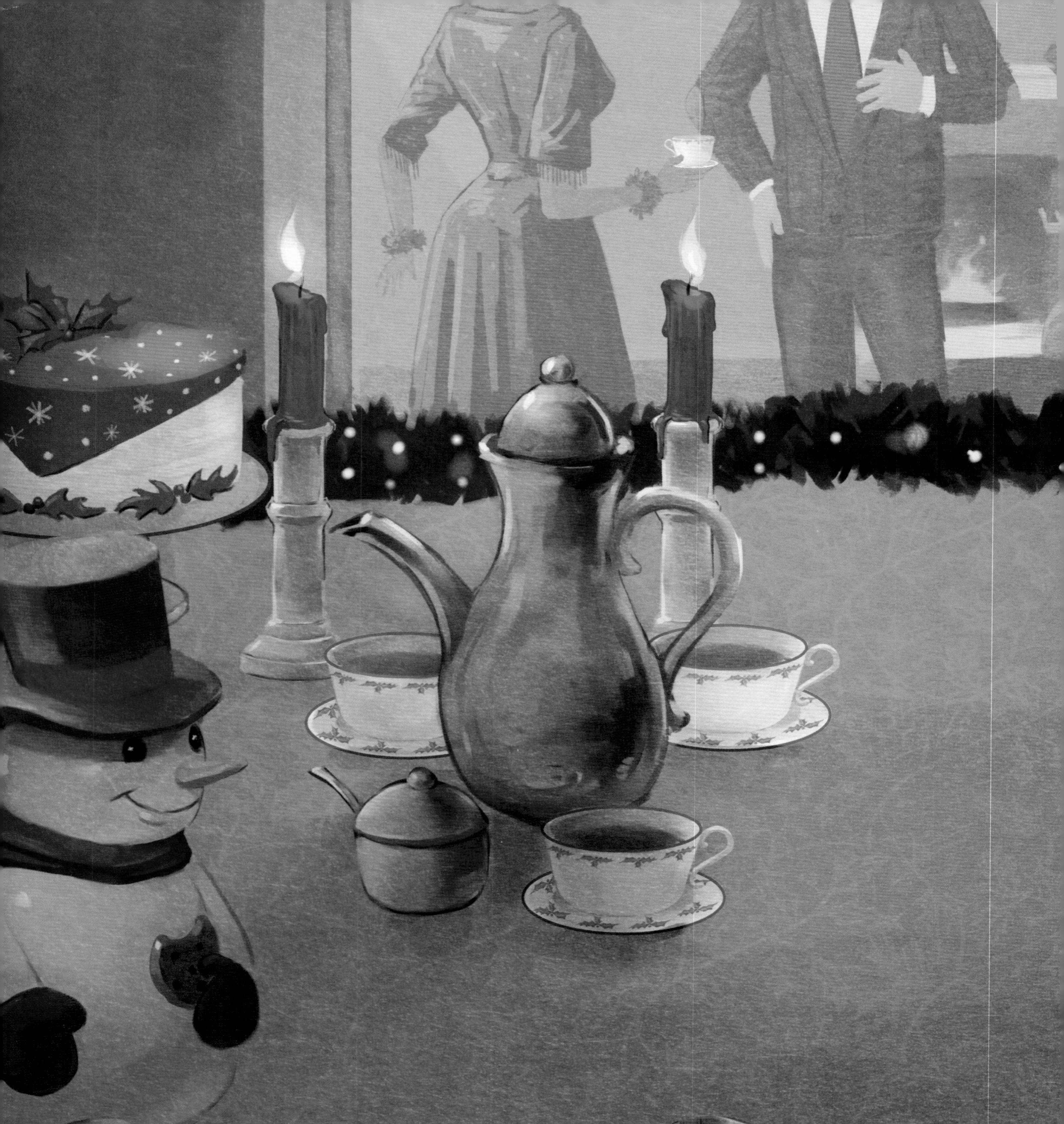

IN A COOKIE SWAP, EVERYONE BRINGS A BUNCH OF A FAVORITE COOKIE TO SHARE AND THEN GOES HOME WITH A TIN FILLED WITH ALL THE DIFFERENT COOKIES.

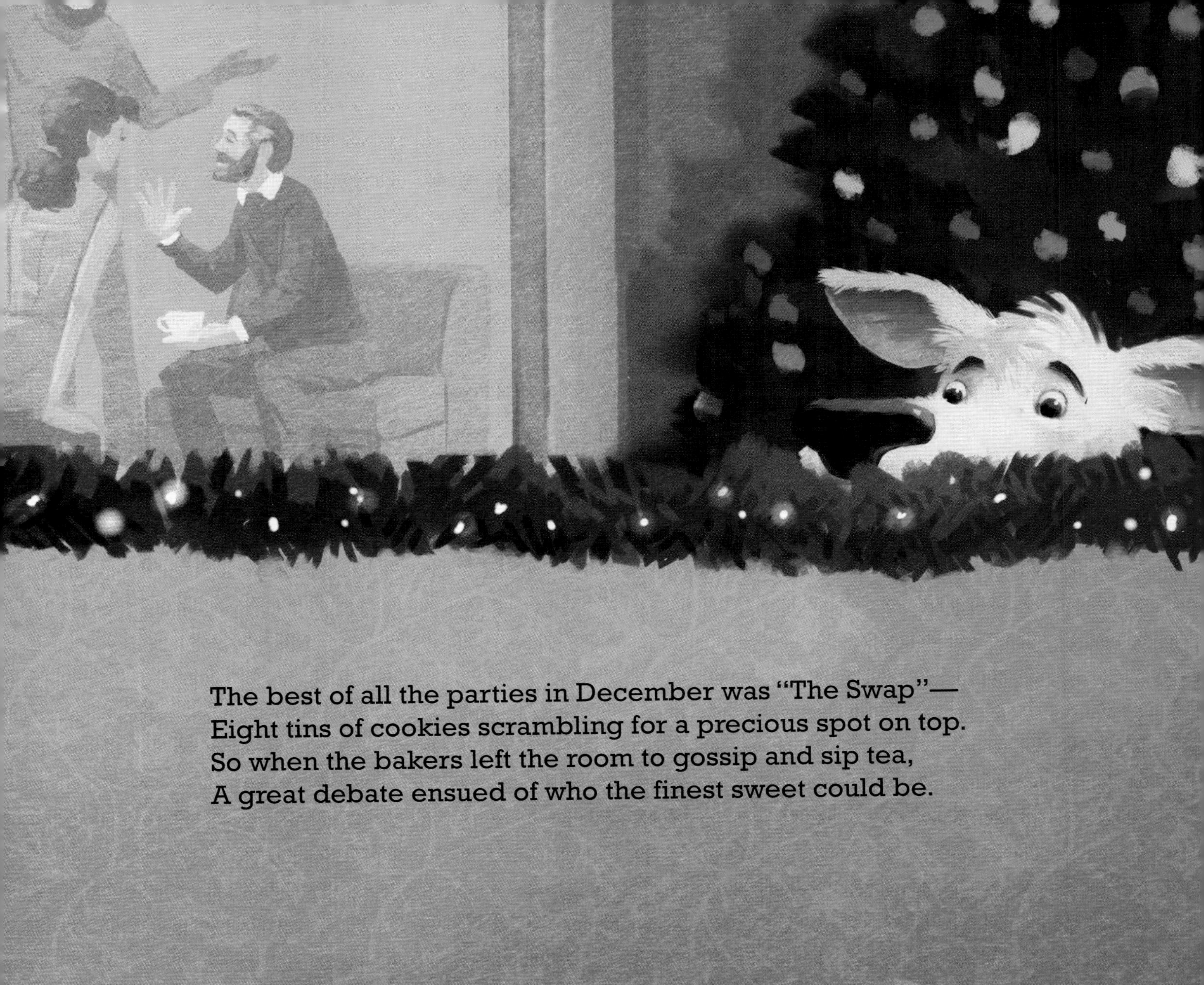

The best of all the parties in December was "The Swap"—
Eight tins of cookies scrambling for a precious spot on top.
So when the bakers left the room to gossip and sip tea,
A great debate ensued of who the finest sweet could be.

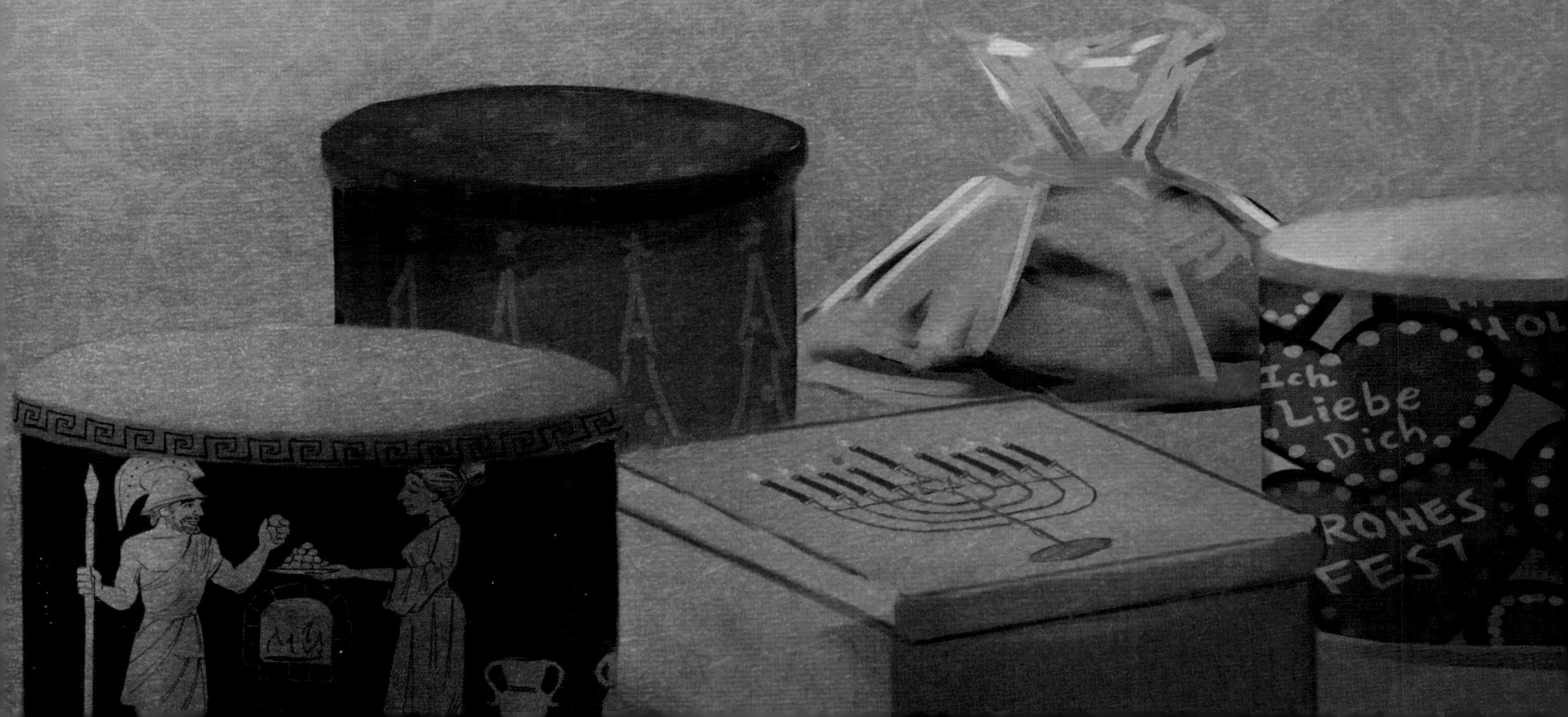
Ich
Liebe
Dich
FEST

The first to rise was Ya-Ya, sugar-
  dusted, plump, and Greek.
"My recipe's by far the oldest—
  mine's the treat they seek!
My nutty butter sweetness makes the
  perfect party bite."
"Oh, Grandma, please," a voice
  came forth. "I've lost my appetite!"

YA-YA (GREEK FOR "GRANDMOTHER") IS RIGHT:
KOURABIEDES ARE THE OLDEST COOKIES IN
THIS BOOK, DATING FROM 1200 B.C.

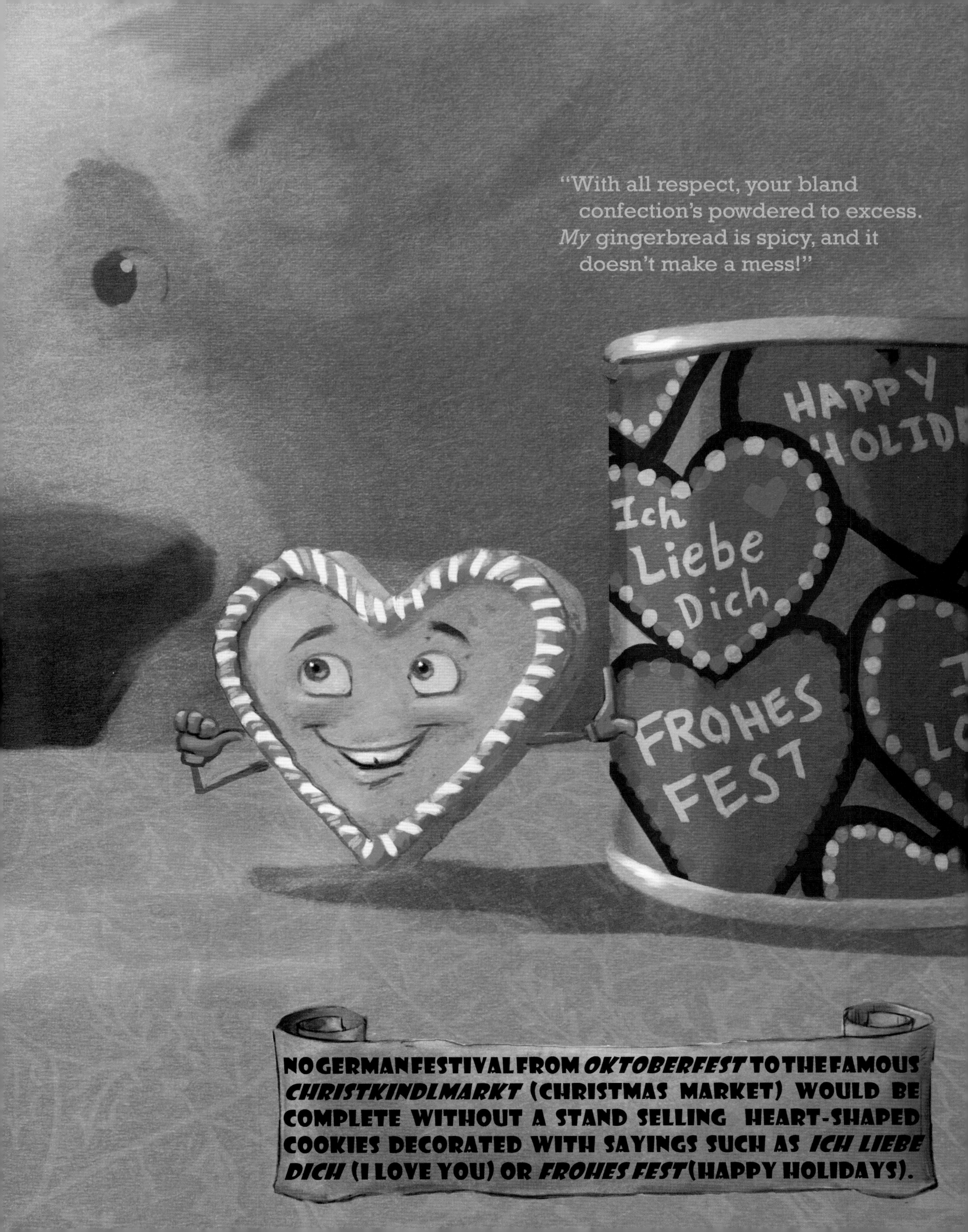
HAPPY HOLIDA
Ich Liebe Dich
FROHES FEST

"With all respect, your bland
confection's powdered to excess.
My gingerbread is spicy, and it
doesn't make a mess!"

NO GERMAN FESTIVAL FROM *OKTOBERFEST* TO THE FAMOUS *CHRISTKINDLMARKT* (CHRISTMAS MARKET) WOULD BE COMPLETE WITHOUT A STAND SELLING HEART-SHAPED COOKIES DECORATED WITH SAYINGS SUCH AS *ICH LIEBE DICH* (I LOVE YOU) OR *FROHES FEST* (HAPPY HOLIDAYS).

"Oy, mind your elders! Such a kvetch!" cried Mrs. Mandelbrot.
"Your heart may well be tasty, but I strike a better note.
At Hanukkah, my twice-baked treat goes perfectly with tea."
The Benne Wafer piped up then, "Still, not as good as me!"

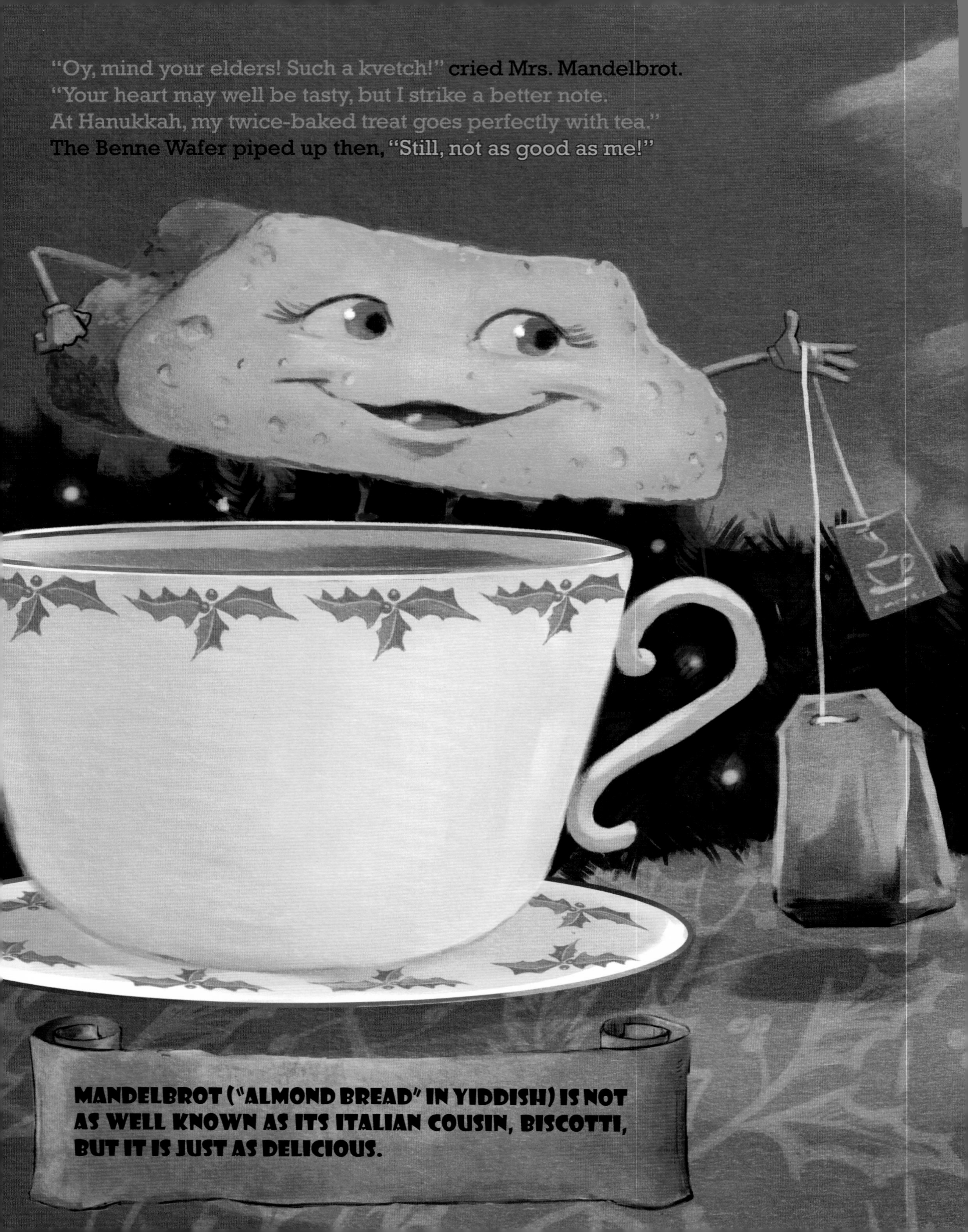

MANDELBROT ("ALMOND BREAD" IN YIDDISH) IS NOT AS WELL KNOWN AS ITS ITALIAN COUSIN, BISCOTTI, BUT IT IS JUST AS DELICIOUS.

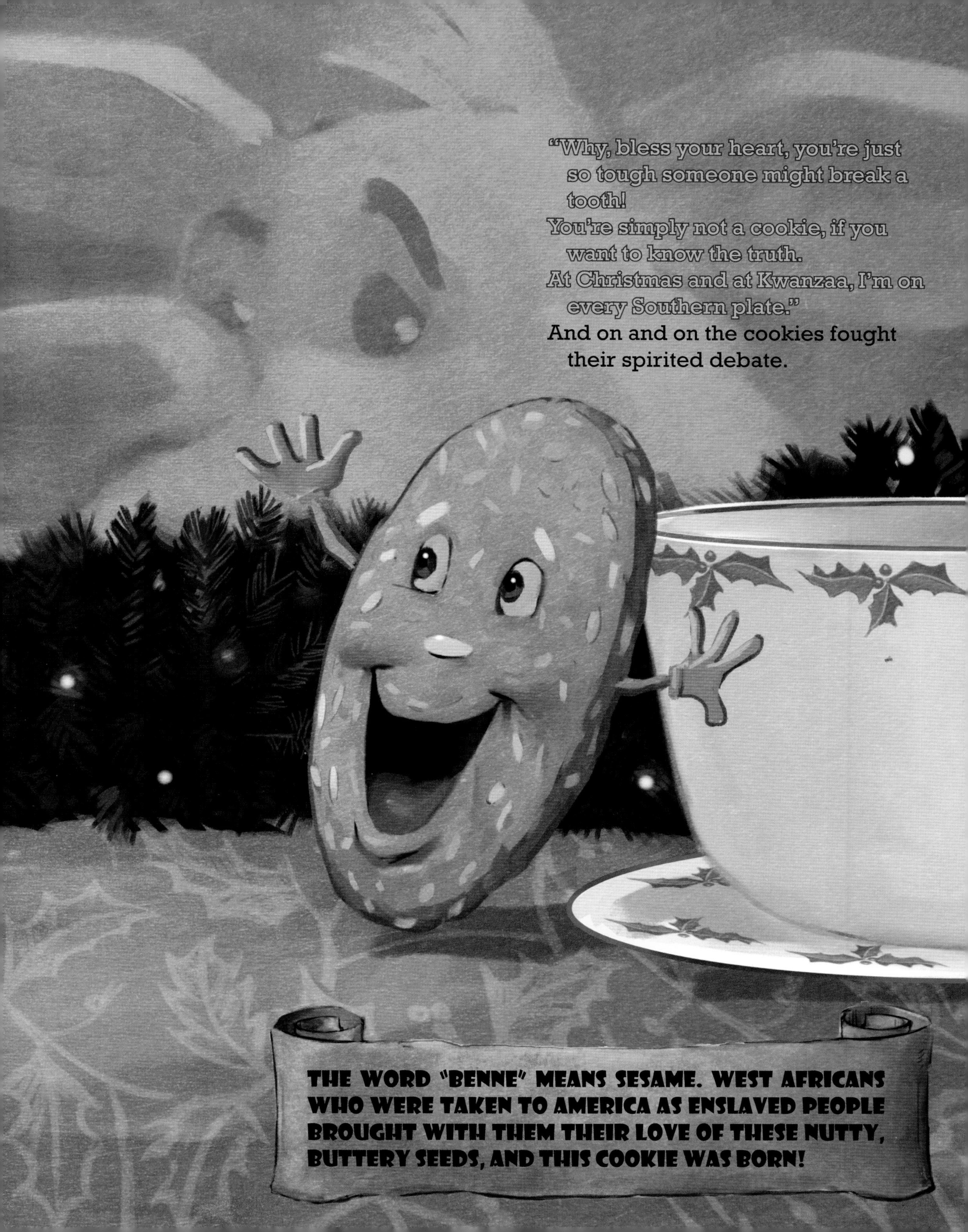

"Why, bless your heart, you're just
so tough someone might break a
tooth!
You're simply not a cookie, if you
want to know the truth.
At Christmas and at Kwanzaa, I'm on
every Southern plate."
And on and on the cookies fought
their spirited debate.

THE WORD "BENNE" MEANS SESAME. WEST AFRICANS WHO WERE TAKEN TO AMERICA AS ENSLAVED PEOPLE BROUGHT WITH THEM THEIR LOVE OF THESE NUTTY, BUTTERY SEEDS, AND THIS COOKIE WAS BORN!

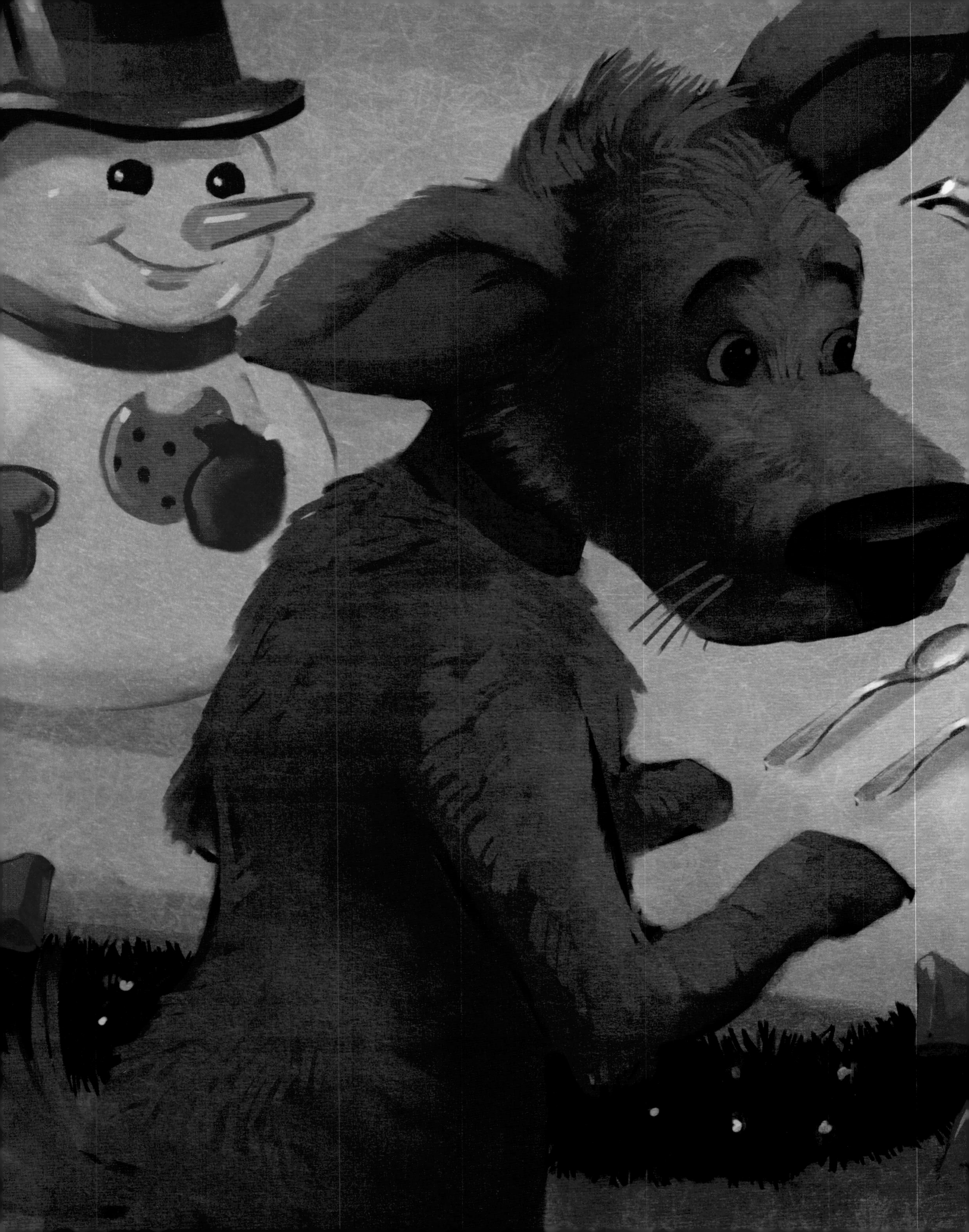

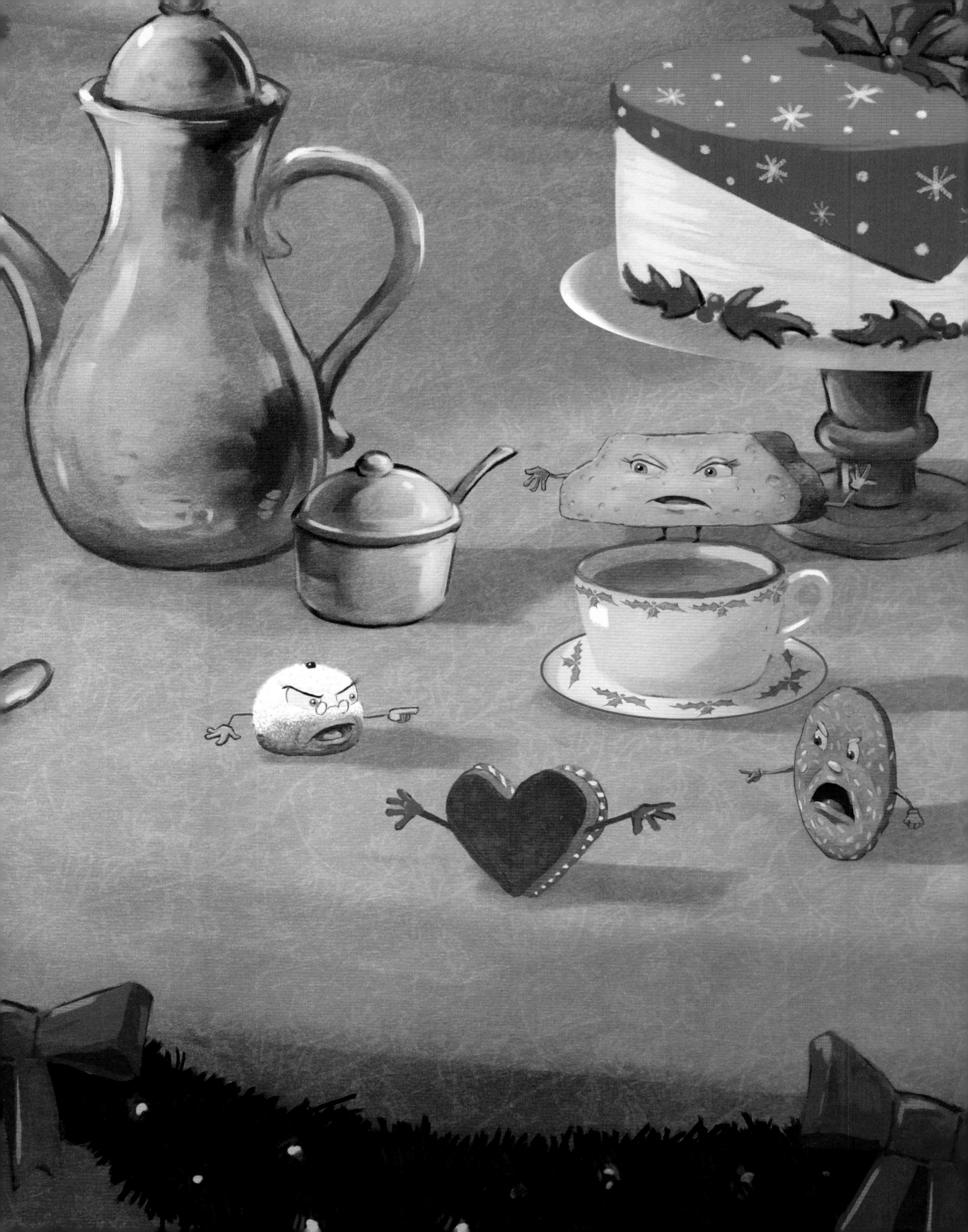

"Now, grandmas, quit yer quarrels,"
came a slow, Midwestern drawl.
"Just step aside, 'cause I'm the finest
festive sweet of all!
A peanut butter center coated with a
chocolate shell?
No one would turn a Buckeye down so
far as I can tell!"

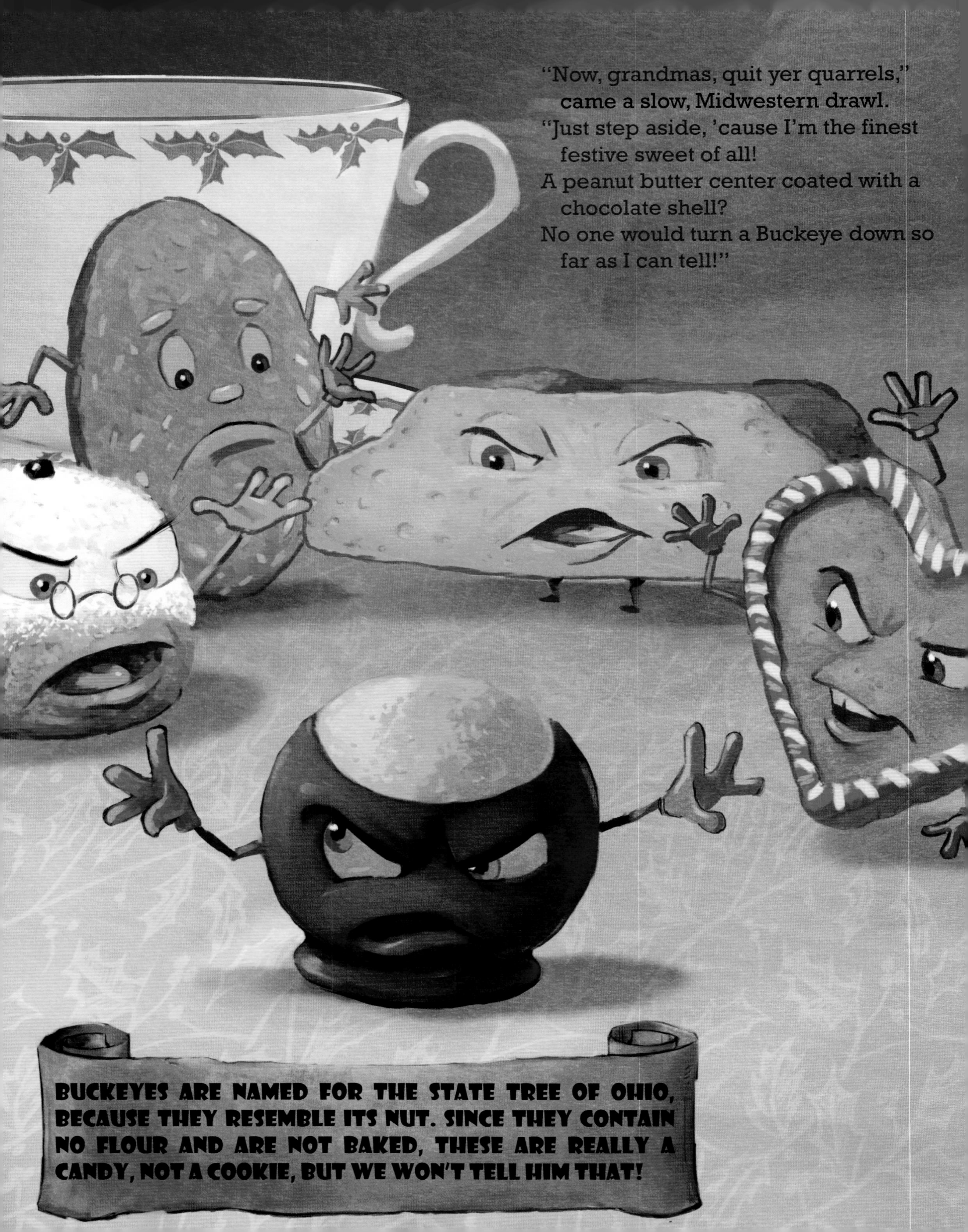

BUCKEYES ARE NAMED FOR THE STATE TREE OF OHIO, BECAUSE THEY RESEMBLE ITS NUT. SINCE THEY CONTAIN NO FLOUR AND ARE NOT BAKED, THESE ARE REALLY A CANDY, NOT A COOKIE, BUT WE WON'T TELL HIM THAT!

"Oh yeah?" **broke in another sweet.** "I fear I disagree!
Why, peanuts are like poison if one has an allergy!
My spicy chocolate crunch is free of nuts and gluten, too.
Your *Navidad* will be *feliz* with just a single chew!"

THESE COOKIES ARE INSPIRED BY THE SPICY FLAVORS OF MEXICAN HOT CHOCOLATE. CHOCOLATE CAN BE TRACED BACK TO THE MAYA AND AZTEC PEOPLES THOUSANDS OF YEARS AGO.

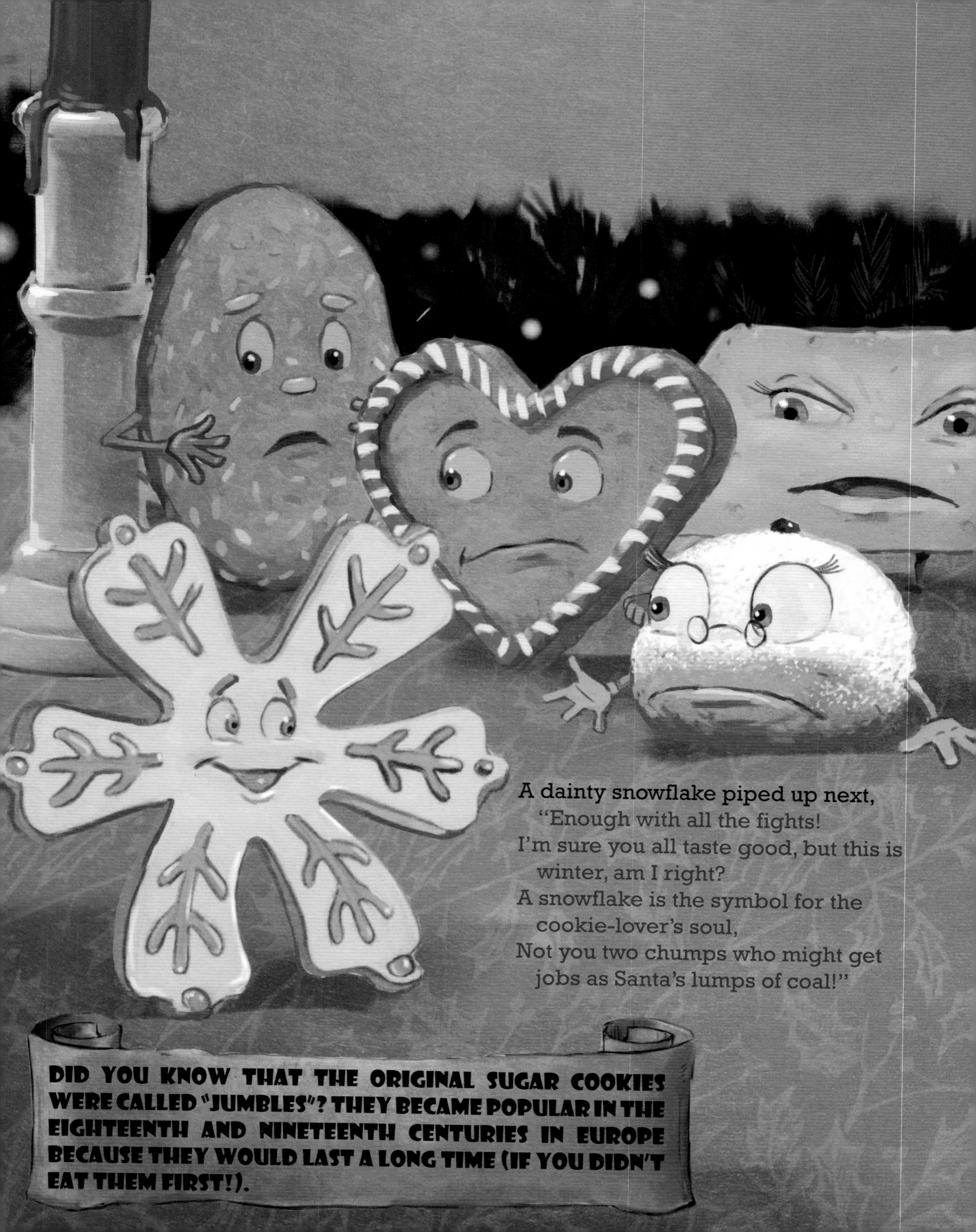

A dainty snowflake piped up next,
"Enough with all the fights!
I'm sure you all taste good, but this is
winter, am I right?
A snowflake is the symbol for the
cookie-lover's soul,
Not you two chumps who might get
jobs as Santa's lumps of coal!"

DID YOU KNOW THAT THE ORIGINAL SUGAR COOKIES WERE CALLED "JUMBLES"? THEY BECAME POPULAR IN THE EIGHTEENTH AND NINETEENTH CENTURIES IN EUROPE BECAUSE THEY WOULD LAST A LONG TIME (IF YOU DIDN'T EAT THEM FIRST!).

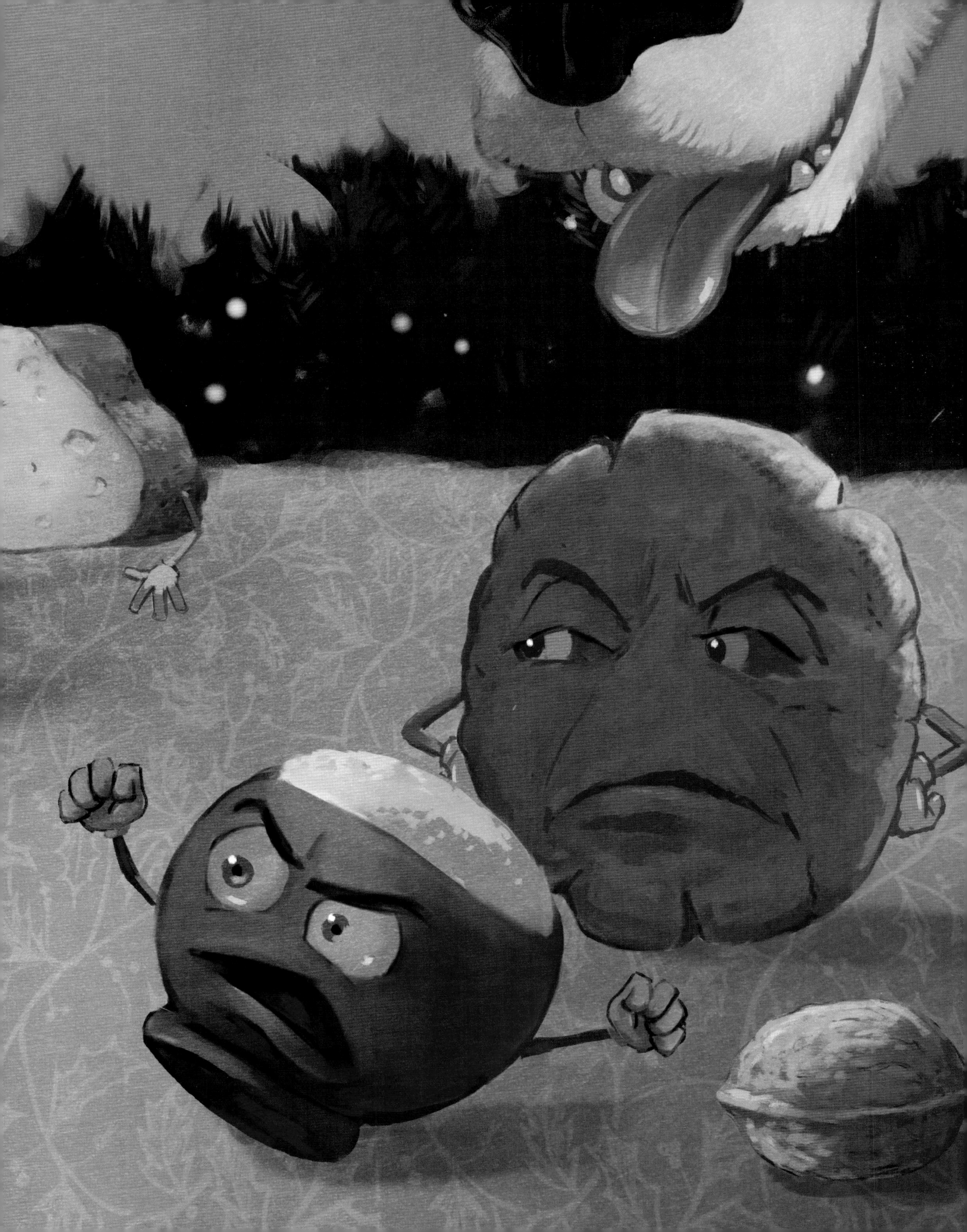

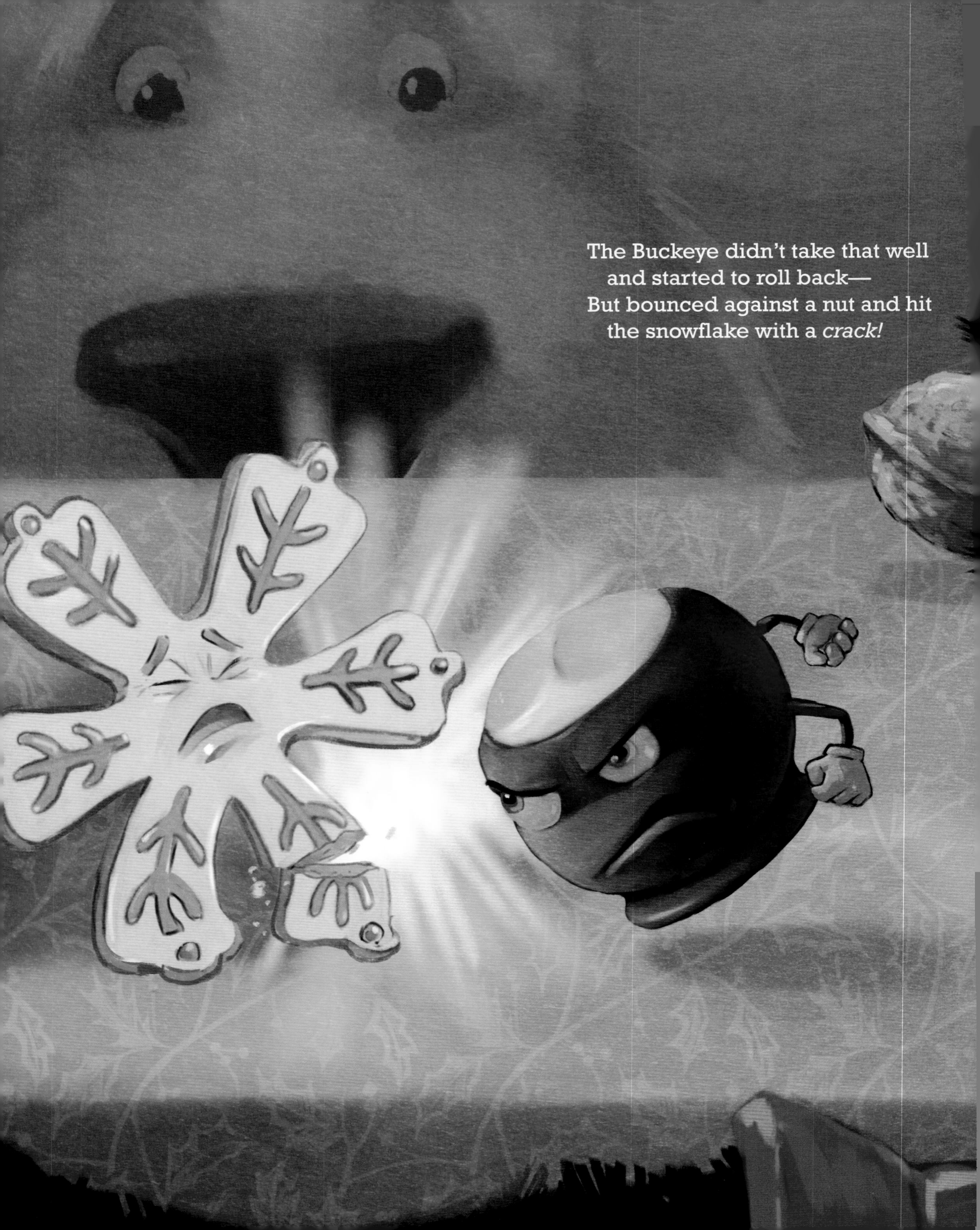

The Buckeye didn't take that well
and started to roll back—
But bounced against a nut and hit
the snowflake with a *crack!*

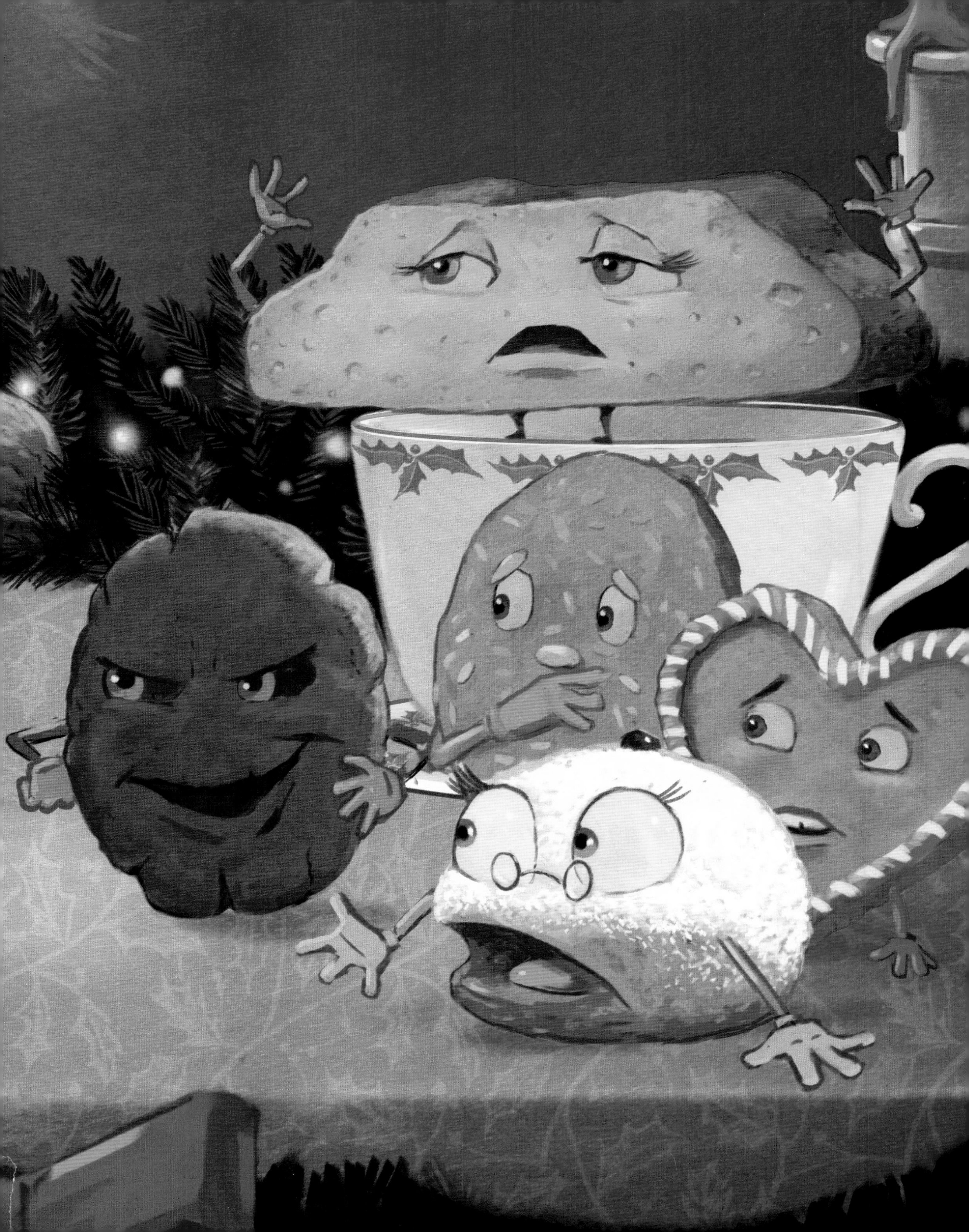

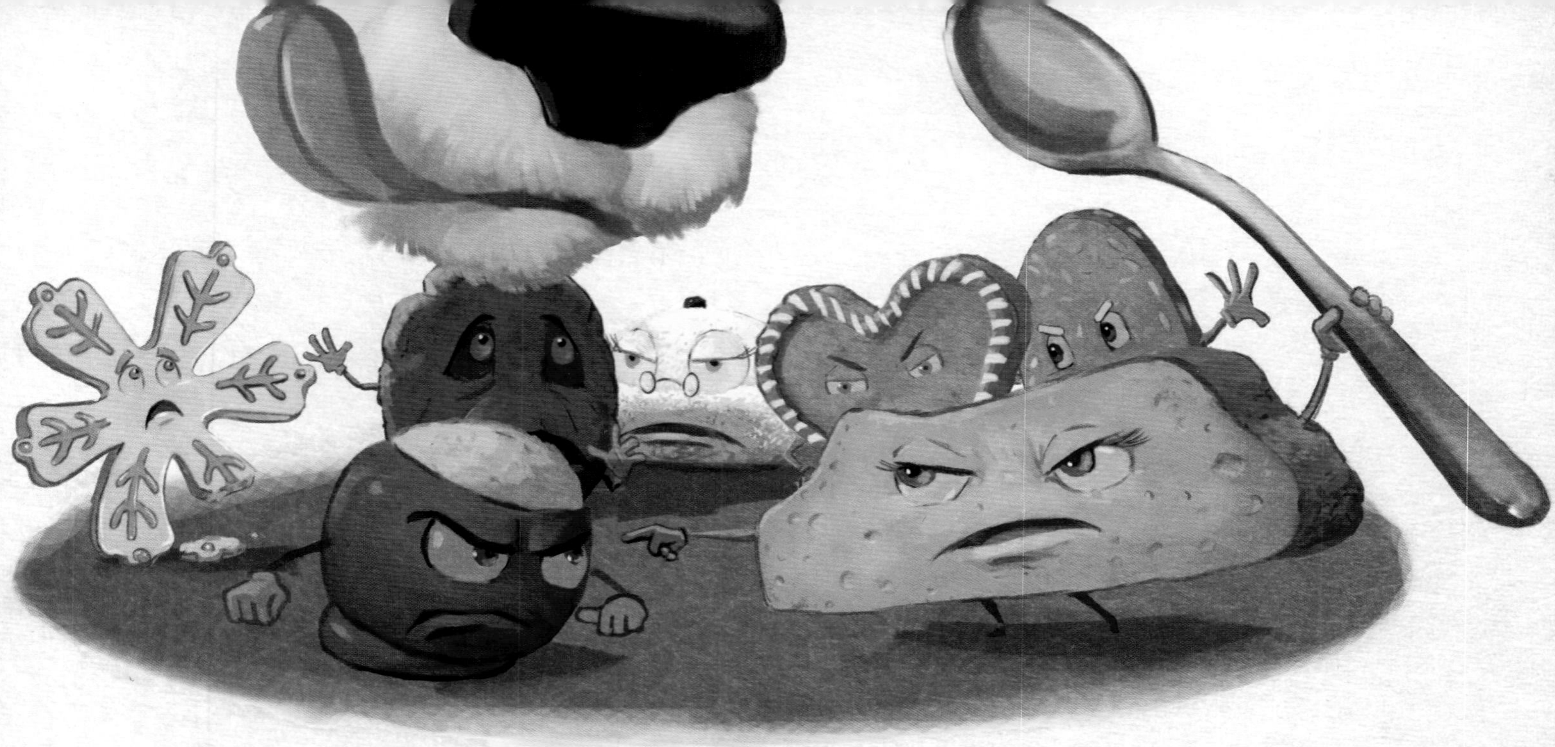

"You bully!" countered Mandelbrot and stepped up to the plate.
A powdered-sugar dustup seemed inevitable fate.

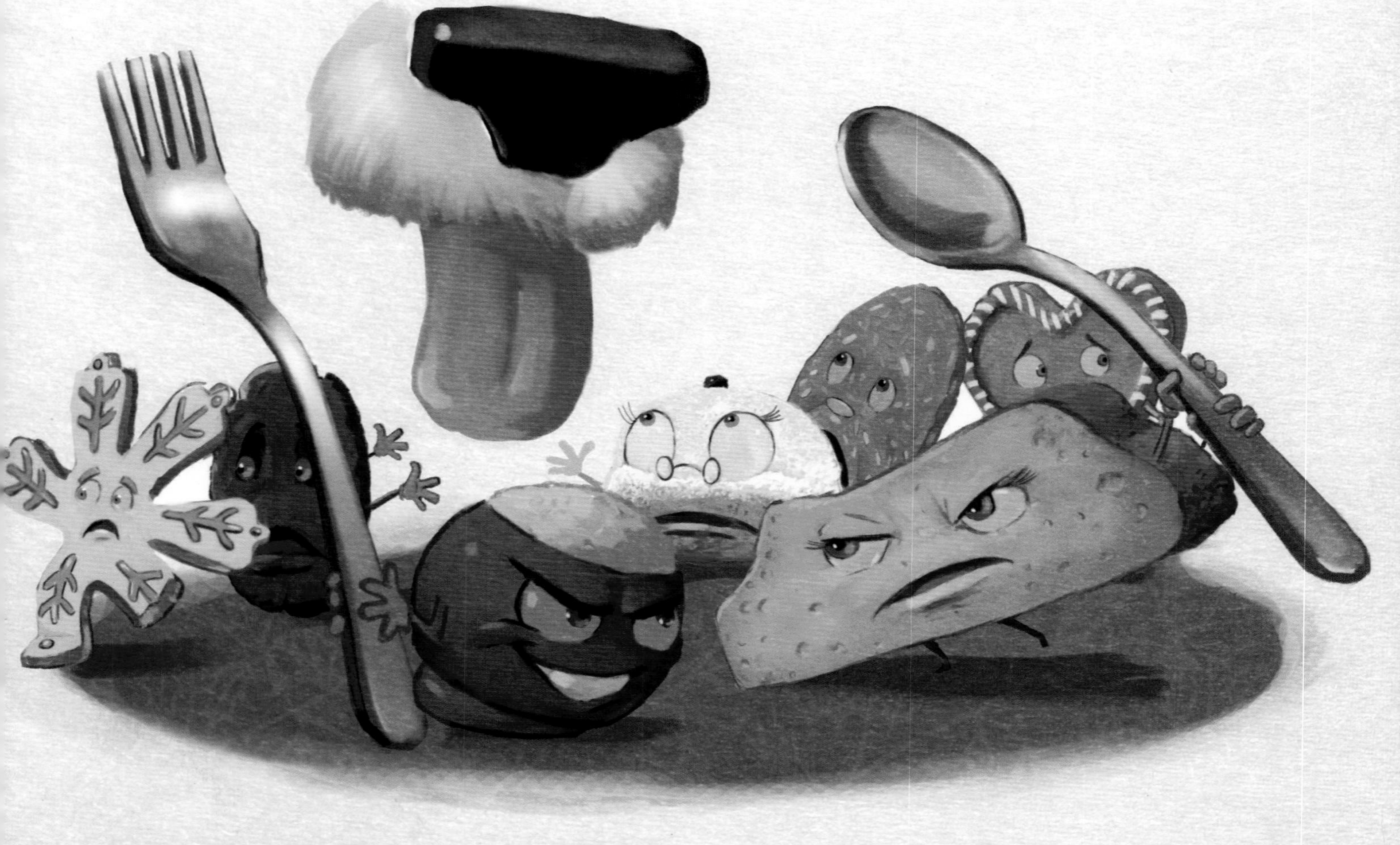

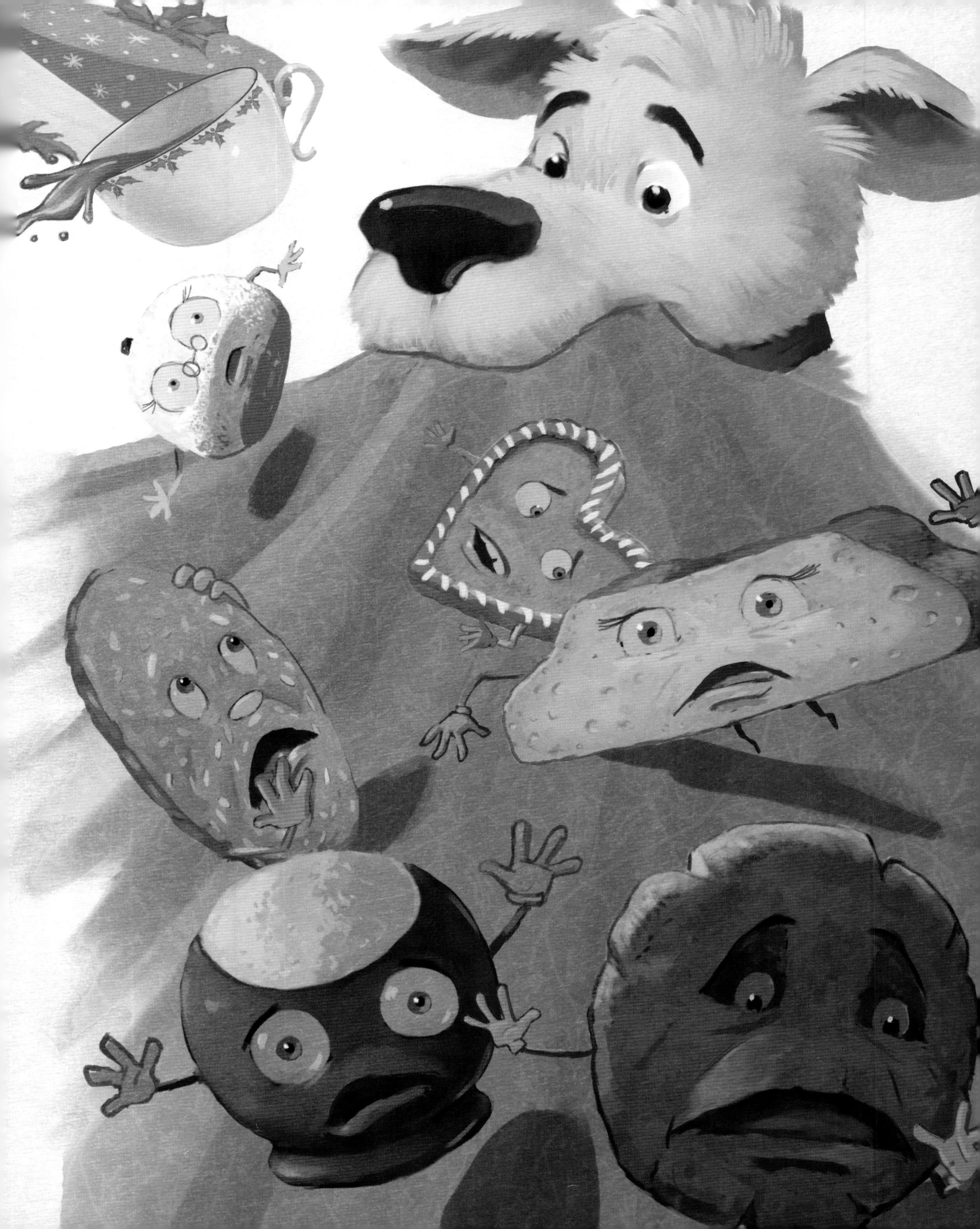

Then from one final tin came an
exasperated sigh:
An old shortbread from India, the kindly
Nan Khatai.
"A fight between two cookies can end
only in their crumbs.
The wiser cookie seeks,
through peace, such hate to
overcome."

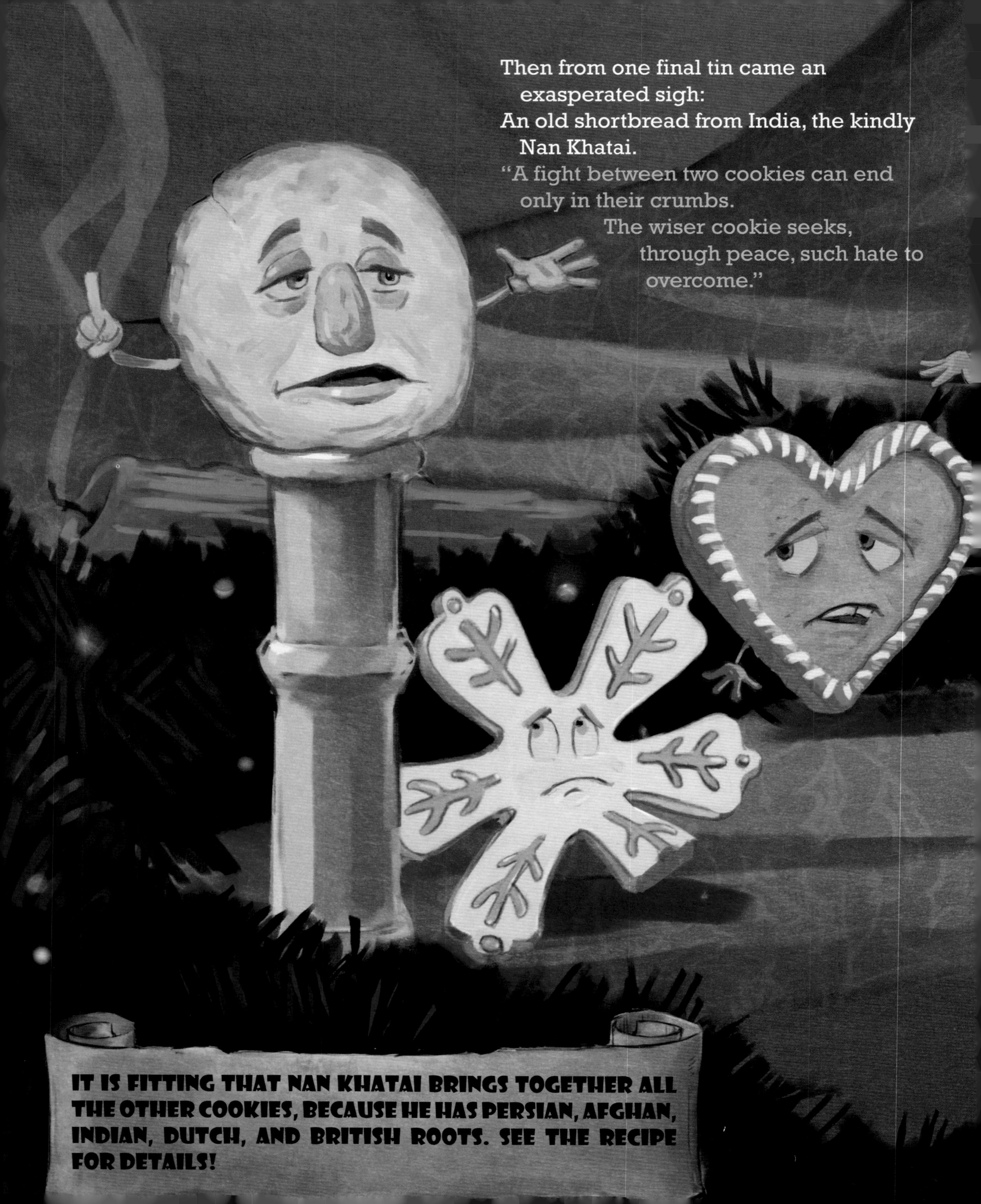

IT IS FITTING THAT NAN KHATAI BRINGS TOGETHER ALL THE OTHER COOKIES, BECAUSE HE HAS PERSIAN, AFGHAN, INDIAN, DUTCH, AND BRITISH ROOTS. SEE THE RECIPE FOR DETAILS!

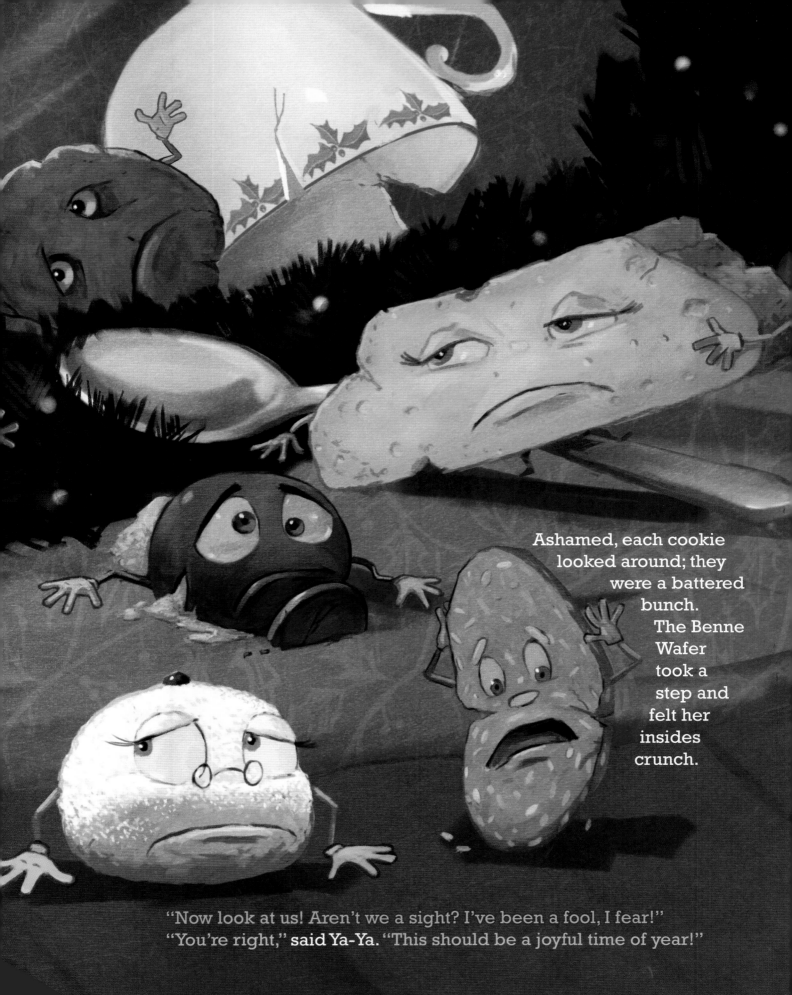

Ashamed, each cookie
looked around; they
were a battered
bunch.
The Benne
Wafer
took a
step and
felt her
insides
crunch.

"Now look at us! Aren't we a sight? I've been a fool, I fear!"
"You're right," said Ya-Ya. "This should be a joyful time of year!"

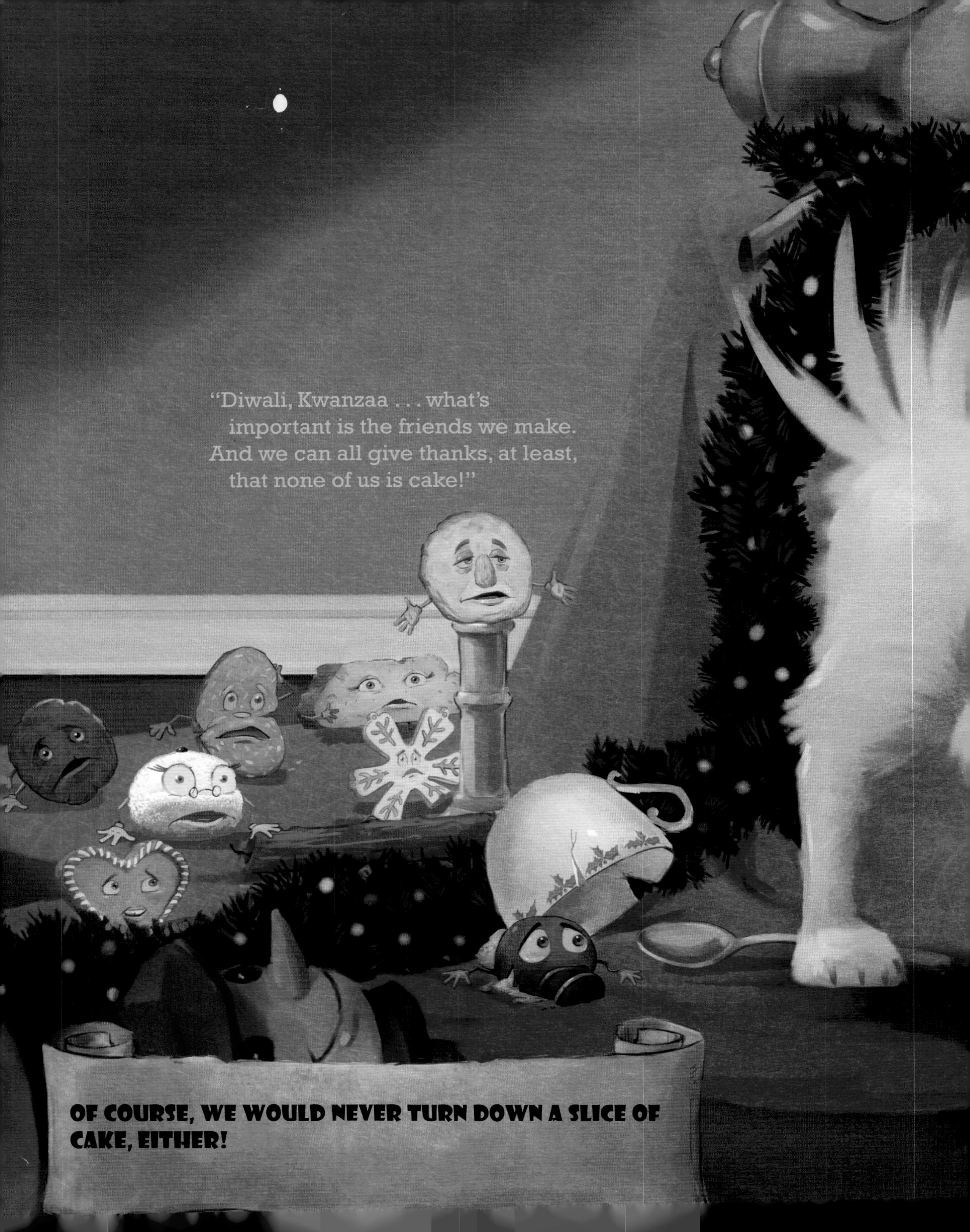

"Diwali, Kwanzaa . . . what's
important is the friends we make.
And we can all give thanks, at least,
that none of us is cake!"

OF COURSE, WE WOULD NEVER TURN DOWN A SLICE OF CAKE, EITHER!

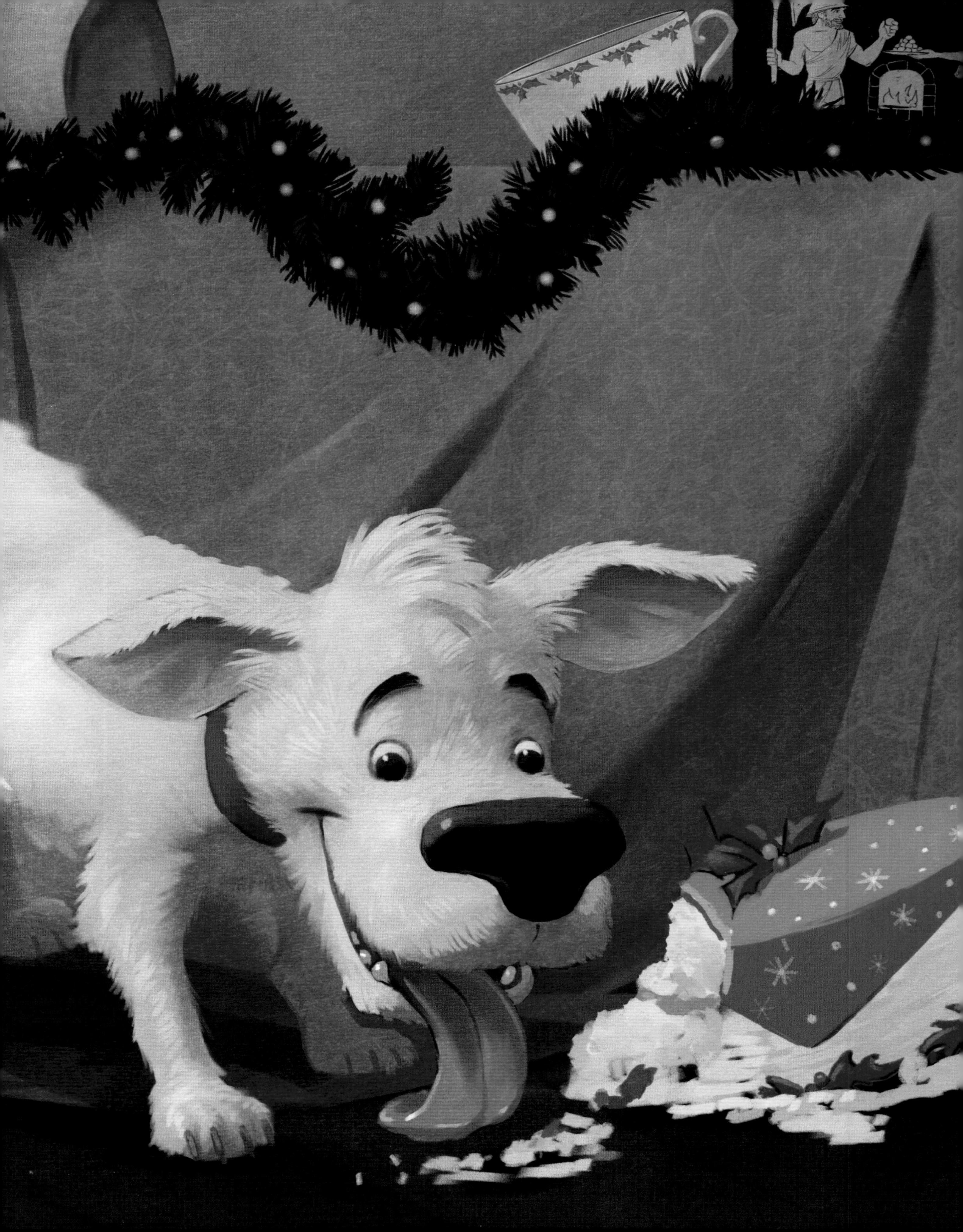

Our Cast of Characters (the Cookies) and How to Make Them

Kourabiedes (Greece)

These buttery cookies (pronounced koo-rah-BEE-eh-dess) are most commonly made with almonds, but walnuts are a variation that makes them a little more sassy, like Ya-Ya. At Christmastime, a single clove is often placed into the top of the cookie to represent the spices brought by the Three Wise Men.

¾ cup walnuts
½ cup butter, softened
½ cup powdered sugar
1 large egg yolk
1 tbsp. rosewater
1 tsp. vanilla extract
1½ cups all-purpose flour

½ tsp. baking powder
¼ tsp. salt

For Dusting After Baking
1-2 tbsp. rosewater
½ cup powdered sugar

Preheat the oven to 350 degrees.

Toast the walnuts for about 6 minutes or until their smell is sweet and they are just browned. Turn off the oven and remove the nuts. When they have cooled, chop about half of the nuts (you should have about ½ cup chopped). Pulse the remaining nuts in a food processor until finely ground.

Using an electric mixer on medium-high speed, cream the butter, sugar, egg yolk, rosewater, and vanilla together until light and fluffy. Gradually mix in the rest of the cookie ingredients, nuts last. The dough may be crumbly. Rest the dough, covered, for 1 hour at room temperature.

Roll the dough into 1-inch balls and place at least 1 inch apart on parchment-lined or greased cookie sheets. Bake at 350 degrees for about 18 minutes or until just browned. Remove cookies from the oven and flick rosewater over them with a pastry brush or your fingers (wash your hands first!). Don't use too much—rosewater can be very strong!

Put the powdered sugar in a zip-top bag and add 5 to 6 of the warm cookies to it. Shake the bag gently until the cookies are coated with sugar. Repeat with the rest of the cookies. Yield: About 2 dozen.

Lebkuchenherzen (Germany)

Traditional recipes for this German gingerbread (pronounced layb-koo-ken-HAIR-tsen) always include honey and cloves. Our recipe adds molasses but no refined sugar, something many people like to avoid. The royal icing does contain refined sugar, however, so if that is a concern for you, try this alternate version: before baking, brush cookies with egg white for a glossy finish. (You can also add whole or slivered almonds in a pattern on top for a more interesting presentation.)

¾ cup molasses
½ cup honey
¾ cup butter, softened
1 tbsp. ground ginger
1 tsp. cinnamon
½ tsp. ground cloves
1 tsp. grated lemon zest
½ tsp. grated orange zest
2 medium eggs

1 tsp. baking soda
¼ tsp. salt
5 cups flour

Royal Icing
⅓ cup liquid egg whites
2 tsp. fresh lemon juice
3 cups powdered sugar

Place molasses and honey in a microwave-safe bowl and microwave on high at 30-second intervals until just bubbling. Cool for 10 minutes. While the molasses and honey are cooling, using an electric mixer, whip the butter with the spices and zests until fluffy and smooth.

Stir molasses and honey mixture into the butter mixture, then beat in eggs, baking soda, and salt. Gradually add the flour, 1 cup at a time, until you get a dough that can almost hold its shape in a ball (it should take about 5 cups). Chill the dough, covered, for at least 1 hour.

Roll dough to ⅓-inch thickness and cut using heart-shaped cookie cutters. Bake on a greased cookie sheet at 350 degrees for 11-13 minutes (do not overbake!). Cool for 10 minutes.

To make the icing, whip egg whites with an electric mixer until soft peaks form. Mix in lemon juice, then gradually mix in sugar until stiff. Pipe a simple border or other decorations on the cooled cookies. Yield: About 3 dozen 2-inch hearts.

Mandelbrot (Eastern Europe)

Like biscotti ("twice baked" in Italian), Jewish mandelbrot cookies (pronounced MAN-dell-broht) are baked twice but are traditionally a little softer and more chewy. If you like a crisper cookie, just bake a minute or two longer at each stage! These cookies can also be dipped in chocolate, but if you follow Jewish dietary laws, watch for the presence of dairy.

1 cup vegetable oil
1 cup sugar
3 large eggs
1 tsp. vanilla extract

1 tsp. salt
3 cups flour
1½ cups sliced or chopped almonds

Using an electric mixer, beat together the oil, sugar, eggs, and vanilla for 3-5 minutes or until thickened and bright yellow. Add the remaining ingredients, and beat until well mixed. Chill the dough, covered, for at least 3 hours or overnight.

Divide the dough in half and form into 2 long logs on 2 greased cookie sheets. Bake at 350 degrees for 25-30 minutes or until just browned. Cool the logs on the sheets for 10 minutes, then remove and slice into ½-inch cookies. Arrange these back on the sheets, reduce the heat to 300 degrees, and bake for another 10 minutes on each side. Yield: About 4 dozen.

Benne Wafers (U.S.)

People are used to seeing sesame seeds on a hamburger bun but . . . in a cookie? Toast them up; add them to some brown sugar, butter, and the other "usual suspects"; and you've got one of the specialties of Charleston, South Carolina. Benne wafers (pronounced BEN-ay) are traditionally made with a tiny scoop, so eat two—they're small!

1 cup white sesame seeds
½ cup butter, softened
1 cup brown sugar
¼ tsp. baking soda

1 tsp. vanilla extract
¼ tsp. salt
1 large egg
1 cup flour

Toast the sesame seeds in a 350-degree oven for about 6 minutes or until just golden. Cool.

Using an electric mixer, cream butter, sugar, baking soda, vanilla, salt, and egg. Add the flour and mix until smooth. Mix in the sesame seeds.

Drop the dough by teaspoonfuls onto greased cookie sheets. (A melon baller size scoop gives the right size—they will look small, but that's OK!) Leave at least 2 inches between the cookies, because they will spread as they bake.

Bake at 350 degrees for about 8 minutes until they look set. Carefully remove from the cookie sheets and cool on wire racks. The cookies will freeze well but should be frozen in containers to prevent crumbling. Yield: About 4 dozen 2-inch cookies.

Buckeyes (U.S.)

Buckeyes can be a great gluten-free choice, but just because there's no flour doesn't always mean you're home free. Always read labels, even on "innocent" foods such as chocolate chips and peanut butter!

In this recipe, you can use either creamy or crunchy peanut butter, but be careful with natural peanut butter, as it can separate. You may substitute margarine or coconut oil for the butter and dark or milk chocolate chips for semisweet.

16 oz. peanut butter
2½ cups powdered sugar
½ cup butter, softened

1 tsp. vanilla extract
12 oz. semisweet chocolate chips

Mix peanut butter, sugar, butter, and vanilla until semi-dry and crumbly. Shape by hand into ½-inch balls. Refrigerate them while you prepare the chocolate.

Melt the chocolate chips in a microwave-safe bowl. Dip balls into chocolate (a toothpick or skewer works well . . . but will leave a little hole in the top). Leave a bit of the peanut butter exposed at the top to look like a buckeye nut.

Place on a wax-paper-lined tray and refrigerate until set. Refrigeration recommended for storage but not required. They also freeze well! Yield: 4-5 dozen.

Mexican Hot Chocolate Cookies (Mexico)

These cookies are inspired by Mexican hot chocolate, which is made with cinnamon and chili powder. They are another gluten-free option. Their spicy bite will warm you up at holiday celebrations, whether you live where it's cold or in the sunny South!

1½ cups powdered sugar
½ cup dark cocoa powder
1½ tsp. cinnamon
½ tsp. chili powder (or ancho chile powder)
¼ tsp. salt

1 tsp. cornstarch
1-3 egg whites (or 3-9 tbsp. liquid egg whites)
1 tsp. vanilla extract
1 cup semisweet chocolate chips

Preheat the oven to 350 degrees.

Whisk together powdered sugar, cocoa powder, cinnamon, chili powder, salt, and cornstarch. Add 1 egg white (or 3 tbsp. liquid whites) and vanilla, and mix until thoroughly combined. Add more egg white gradually, until the mixture is like fudgy brownie batter. If you add too much egg white, they will still be fine but will spread more.

Stir in the chocolate chips. Drop by spoonfuls at least 1 inch apart on a parchment-lined cookie sheet (the cookies will spread). Parchment is essential here for a well-formed cookie. Bake for 14 minutes. Let cookies cool on the parchment before removing. Yield: About 18 3-inch cookies.

Sugar Cookies (U.S.)

Modern sugar cookies can be traced to the Amish in Pennsylvania, who are well known for their delicious desserts. Since the cookies are easily cut out, they can be made into any holiday shape, not just snowflakes! While there are lots of sugar cookie recipes, this one uses orange extract instead of the traditional vanilla, to give an unexpected subtle zing.

1 cup butter, softened
1 cup sugar
1 large egg

2 tsp. orange extract
1 tsp. baking powder
3 cups flour

Preheat the oven to 350 degrees.

Using an electric mixer, beat the butter and sugar until pale and creamy. Add the egg and extract. Add the baking powder. Gradually add the flour. (The dough will get thick!)

Roll the dough to ¼-inch thickness and cut with a snowflake cutter. Bake on a greased cookie sheet for 6-8 minutes. Cool the cookies on the sheet for 2 minutes, then remove to a wire rack. Yield: About 2 dozen 4-inch cookies.

Nan Khatai (India)

The name "Nan Khatai" (pronounced nahn kah-TIE) comes from the Persian word for bread (naan) and the Afghan word for biscuit (khatai). This cookie's complicated history started when the Indians removed the leavening (yeast) from the bread recipes that Dutch traders left behind. Years later, the shortbread-style treat became popular with the many British who lived in India. Traditionally made with ghee (clarified butter), it can also be made with coconut oil for a vegan cookie.

½ cup sugar
½ cup coconut oil, softened butter, or
    ghee
1 cup flour

½ tsp. baking soda
1 tsp. cardamom powder
Whole pistachios or almonds (optional)

Preheat the oven to 350 degrees.

Using an electric mixer, blend the sugar and coconut oil. Gradually mix in the flour, baking soda, and cardamom. Knead by hand when dough gets stiff, just until it holds together.

Roll the dough into 1-inch balls and flatten with your hand. Place about 2 inches apart on a greased cookie sheet. Put a single nut in the middle of each cookie, if desired. Bake for 15-18 minutes (do not overbake!). Yield: About 18 2-inch cookies.

Author's Note

Everyone loves cookies! As a Girl Scout, I sold boxes and boxes of them. I longed for Christmas, when I could help my mother decorate sugar cookies and gingerbread men. For me, the glorious variety of cookies represents the variety of holidays we celebrate in the U.S. and around the world. In this book, I feature cookies from many different cultural traditions and also with a variety of dietary considerations. If I didn't include your favorite cookie, or even your favorite holiday, don't worry—just have a cookie swap with *your* favorite. Happy holidays!

What Holidays Are Celebrated in December?

Holiday	*When is it celebrated?*
Diwali (Hindu)*	Varies but between the end of October and the start of November
Hanukkah (Jewish)	Varies but usually between the end of November and the start of January
Bodhi Day (Buddhist)	December 8
Winter Solstice	December 21
Christmas (Christian)	December 25
Kwanzaa	December 26-January 1
New Year's Eve	December 31
Orthodox Christmas (Christian)	January 7

*Technically Diwali it is *not* a December holiday, but because it is a joyous festival of lights, it has a lot in common with many other holidays here! Nan Khatai are often baked for Diwali.

Note: The Muslim holiday of Eid al-Fitr, somewhat similar to the celebrations listed here, is often celebrated with sweets and cookies. However, the dates vary from year to year—it will not be observed in the winter months until 2028 (February 27).